ROSES ON BAKER STREET

EILEEN M. BERRY

ILLUSTRATED BY
JOHN ROBERTS

JOURNEY
BOOKS™

Greenville, South Carolina

Library of Congress Cataloging-in-Publication Data

Berry, Eileen M., 1970-
    Roses on Baker Street   /   Eileen M. Berry ; illustrated by John Roberts.
        p.   cm.
    Summary: Danae, who has grown up in France as the daughter of missionaries, has to move with them to America and finds herself in an unfamiliar and strange place when she goes to school there.
    ISBN 0-89084-934-X
    [1. Moving, Household—Fiction. 2. Schools—Fiction.
3. Missionaries—Fiction.]   I. Roberts, John, 1950-   ill.
II. Title.
PZ7.B46168Ro   1998
[E]—dc21   97–47278
                                                 CIP
                                                    AC

Roses on Baker Street

Project Editor: Debbie L. Parker
Designed by Roger Bruckner

© 1998 Journey Books
Published by Bob Jones University Press
Greenville, South Carolina 29614

ISBN 0-89084-934-X

15 14 13 12 11 10 9 8 7 6 5 4 3 2 1

For Mom,
who helps me look for roses.
—EB

To my wonderful children:
Melanie, Jared, Joseph, Seth, and Daniel
—JR

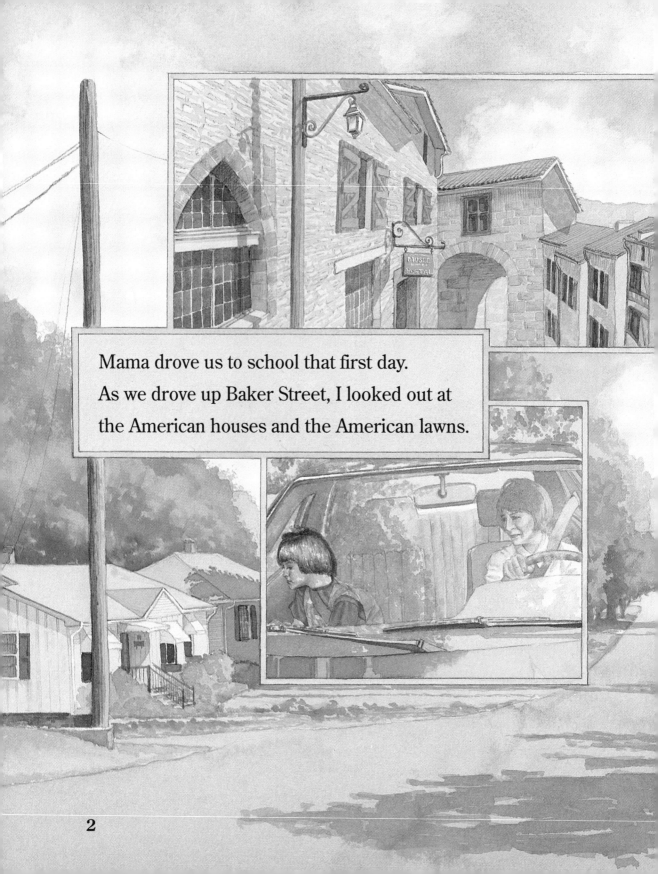

Mama drove us to school that first day.
As we drove up Baker Street, I looked out at
the American houses and the American lawns.

There were no roses
wandering up stone walls.
There were no sheets of lace
fluttering at open windows.
There was no village church
with a bell tower.
There wasn't a single
person carrying a long
skinny loaf of bread.

I knew I was far from home.

The American school was bigger than my school in France. I found my desk in the back row of the class.

The girl on my right folded the pleats
of her plaid skirt into a fan.
The girl on my left twirled
her long blonde braid around her finger.
The boy in front of me pooched out his lips
and tried to balance his pencil on them.

I sat still, like a rabbit sits
while it is deciding whether to run.

Mrs. Blimm's eyes looked as if she knew
a wonderful secret.
"Class, Danae has come a long way to be with us,"
she said. "Danae, please tell the class where your family
lives and what they do."

6

The two girls looked at me.
The boy turned all the way around in his chair
and dropped the pencil.

I stood. "My family is American," I said.

"But we live in France to tell people there about Jesus.

My papa pastors a church in our village.

But we came back to America to rest this year.

We moved into a house on Baker Street."

8

"Who would like to ask Danae a question?"
Mrs. Blimm asked.

10

The girl in the plaid skirt raised her hand.
"Do you speak French?"

"Yes."

The girl with the blonde braid was next.
"Do you have a best friend in France?"

"Yes. Corinne is her name. She's French."

Even the boy had a question.
"Your name's hard to remember.
Do you have a nickname?"

I wrinkled my eyebrows and thought. "Not an everyday one. But my papa has a special name for me. He calls me *mon petit chou.*"

"What does it mean?"

My face felt hot—even my ears.
"In English it's not the same. It means—
my little cabbage."

13

The girl in the plaid skirt giggled.

The girl with the blonde braid giggled.

In a moment more, the whole class was giggling.

I sat down, feeling small.

"In France, those words mean *sweetheart*," said Mrs. Blimm. "Thank you, Danae, for telling us your special name."

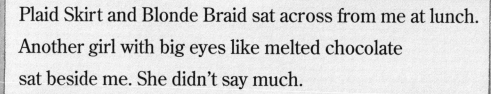

Plaid Skirt and Blonde Braid sat across from me at lunch. Another girl with big eyes like melted chocolate sat beside me. She didn't say much.

Plaid Skirt stood up to peer into my lunch box. "Do you have French food in there?"

"No. A sandwich on American bread."
I took a bite of bologna and cheese.

"Do you like it?" asked Blonde Braid.

"Not as much as French bread.
French bread is thick and hard on the outside.
It makes you chew more."

Plaid Skirt and Blonde Braid looked at each other
and giggled. Chocolate Eyes smiled at me.

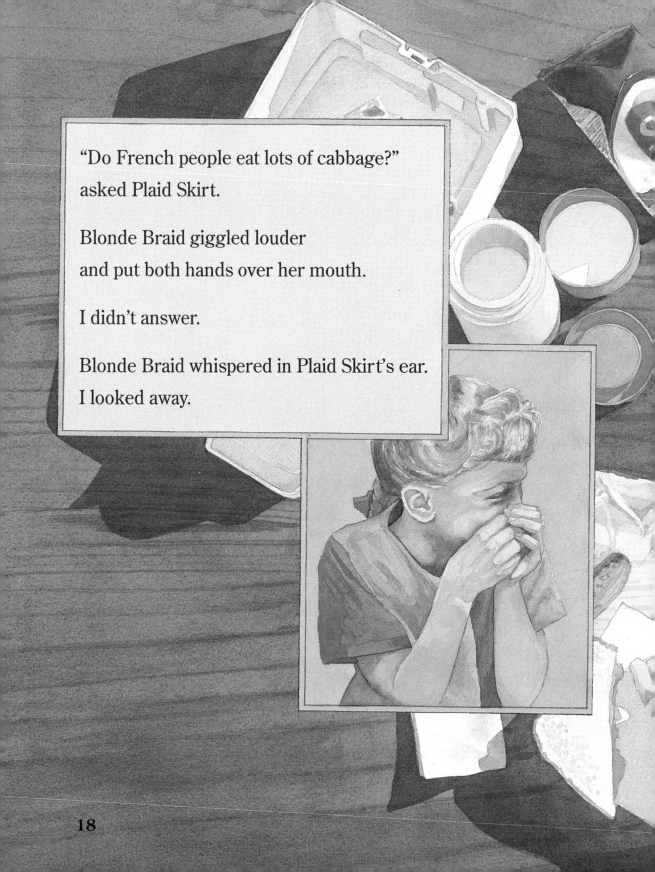

"Do French people eat lots of cabbage?"
asked Plaid Skirt.

Blonde Braid giggled louder
and put both hands over her mouth.

I didn't answer.

Blonde Braid whispered in Plaid Skirt's ear.
I looked away.

Corinne and I used to tell secrets.

19

At supper, Papa asked us how we liked school.

My brother shoved his fork
like a snowplow through his potatoes.
He talked about math quizzes
and book reports and soccer.

20

My sister gnawed around and around
and around her ear of corn.
She talked about lockers and flute lessons
and French club.

I nibbled on bread, taking squirrel bites.
I just listened.

Mama asked me to help clear the table.
Papa stayed too.

I passed him with a stack of plates.
He flipped my hair bow.

"What did you think of school, Danae?"

I handed Mama my plates.
"Not much," I said.

"Tell me the names of your new friends," said Mama.

I wrinkled my eyebrows and thought of Plaid Skirt and Blonde Braid and Pencil Boy and Chocolate Eyes. I hadn't even learned their names.

"I don't remember," I said. "But there were no Corinnes."

24

Papa sat down in a kitchen chair.

He pulled me onto his lap, even though I'm big now.

"*Mon petit chou*," he said.
"Changes are hard.
But look for the roses—not the thorns.
Okay? Look for the roses."

I wanted to tell him there were no roses in America—
at least not on Baker Street.
I had already looked.
But I felt like a baseball was stuck in my throat.
I pushed my face against his soft shirt
and said nothing.

The next day I walked to school looking for roses.

I saw tall white flowers around a tree.

27 BAKER ST.

28

I saw ruffly red flowers in a window box.

I saw purple flowers in stone pots on a porch.

But no roses.

29

September 12

At school, Mrs. Blimm wrote
bonjour and *au revoir* on the chalkboard.

bonjour

I told the class that *bonjour* means "good day"
and *au revoir* means "good-bye."

We all laughed when they tried to say the words.
They sounded American.

I learned that Plaid Skirt was Tara.

Blonde Braid was Heather.

Pencil Boy was Matthew.

And Chocolate Eyes was Katie.

No one said anything about cabbage all day.

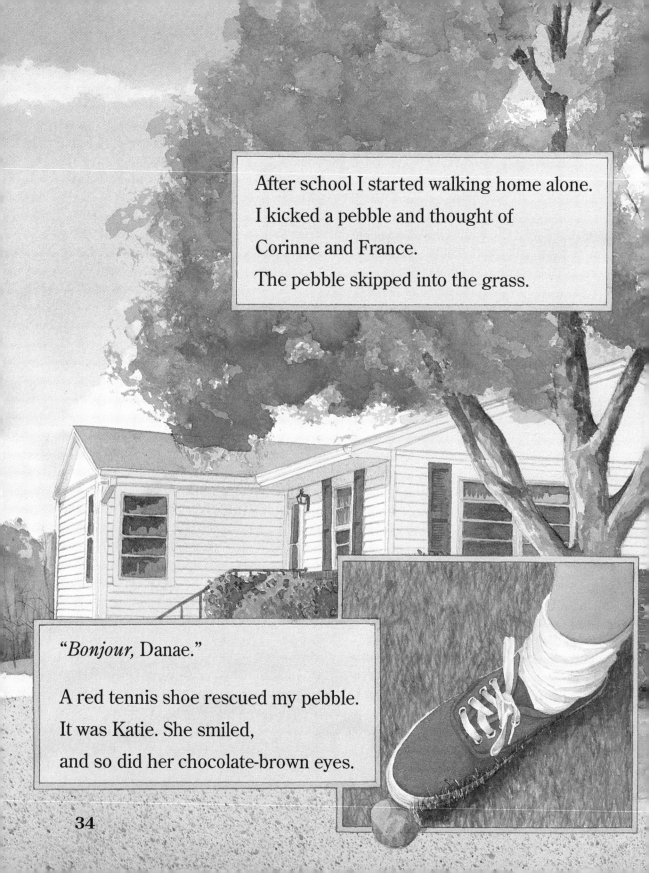

After school I started walking home alone.
I kicked a pebble and thought of
Corinne and France.
The pebble skipped into the grass.

"*Bonjour,* Danae."

A red tennis shoe rescued my pebble.
It was Katie. She smiled,
and so did her chocolate-brown eyes.

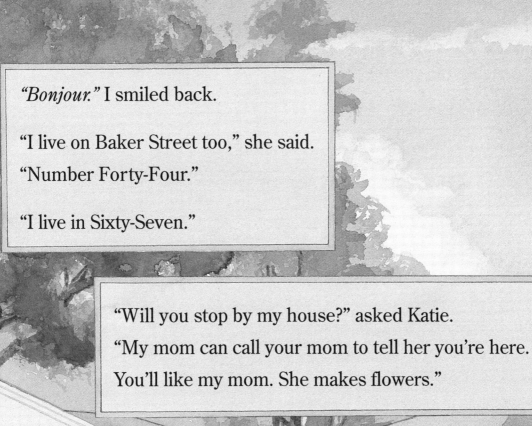

"*Bonjour.*" I smiled back.

"I live on Baker Street too," she said.
"Number Forty-Four."

"I live in Sixty-Seven."

"Will you stop by my house?" asked Katie.
"My mom can call your mom to tell her you're here.
You'll like my mom. She makes flowers."

Outside Katie's house were big, bunchy bushes and a tall tree. But I didn't see any flowers.

Katie's mom didn't come to the door.

Katie ran through the living room,
and I followed.
She ran down the basement steps.
I stopped in the doorway.

37

Everywhere were roses.

Roses swung from ropes on the ceiling.

Roses lay in baskets on the floor.

38

Roses bloomed from glass bowls on a table.

Wreaths of roses hung in rows on every wall.

Red roses, yellow roses, pink roses, purple roses.

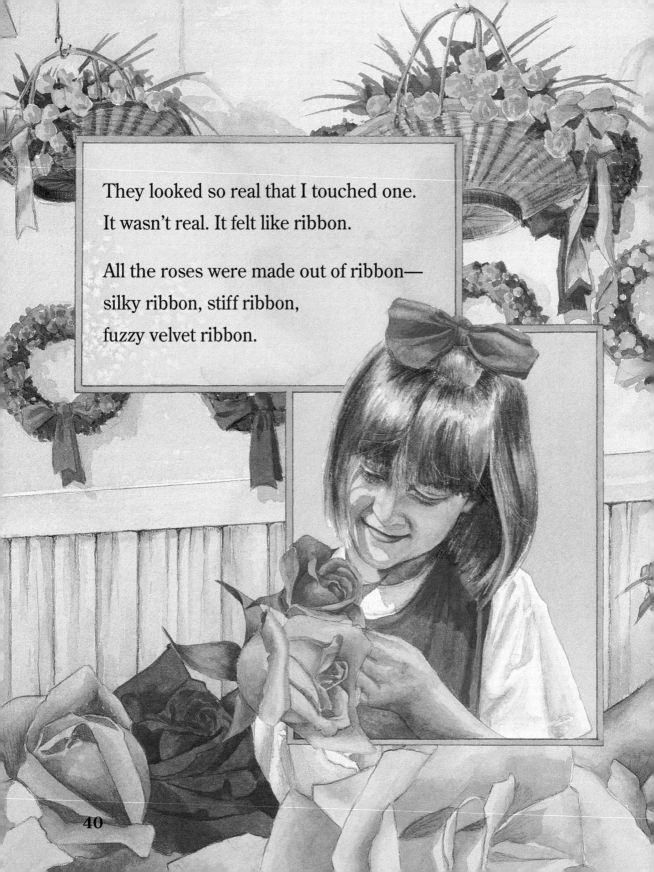

They looked so real that I touched one.
It wasn't real. It felt like ribbon.

All the roses were made out of ribbon—
silky ribbon, stiff ribbon,
fuzzy velvet ribbon.

Katie's mom sat at the table,
winding ribbon around a thin stem
and gluing it in place.
She was making a rose.

Katie whispered to her mother.
Then she grabbed something from the table.

"Mom calls these cabbage roses," she said.
"We wanted you to have one."

She handed me a hair barrette.
It had a big red rose on it, open and full.
The rose looked like it had grown
right there on the barrette.

43

"Thank you," I said.

I pinned the barrette in my hair.

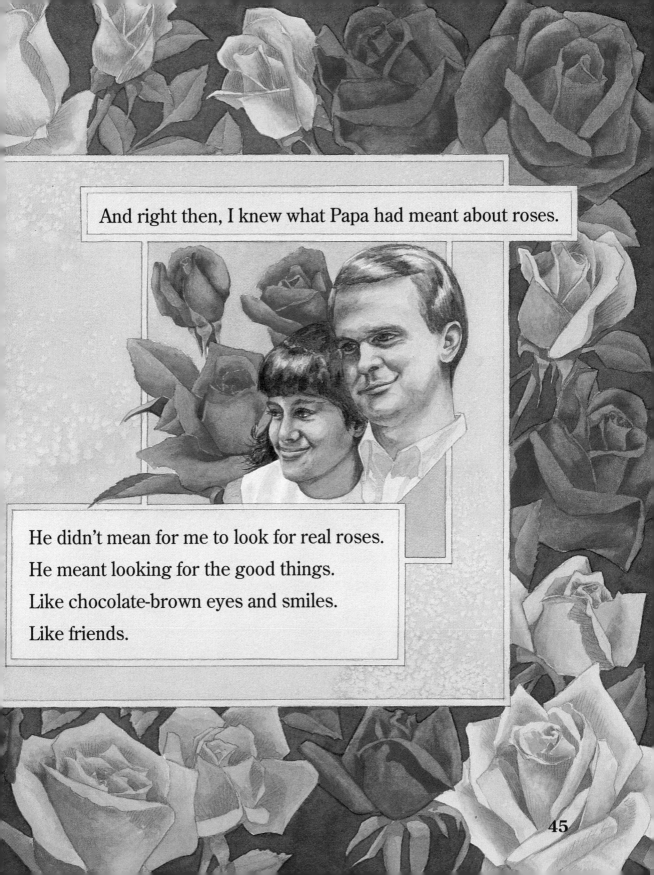

And right then, I knew what Papa had meant about roses.

He didn't mean for me to look for real roses.
He meant looking for the good things.
Like chocolate-brown eyes and smiles.
Like friends.

I couldn't wait to tell Papa.

I had found roses—
right here on Baker Street.